This book is dedicated to Jane Beeby Suwalski,
who told me her story, as well as to friends and family,
whose suggestions helped this book to its present form.
Many thanks to Hollyann M. Brown, Jody Clark, Anne
Houser, Mark Rogers, Matthew Rogers, and Jean Rubin.

The One-Week-Old Fawn: A True Story

Story © 2017 by Suzanne M. Malpass, straddlebooks@gmail.com
Illustrations © 2017 by Trish Morgan, trish@peachbloomhill.com

Requests for permission to excerpt or make copies of any part of the work should be submitted online at info@mascotbooks.com or mailed to Mascot Books, 560 Herndon Parkway #120, Herndon, VA 20170.

PRT0617A

Printed in the United States

Library of Congress Control Number: 2017904211

ISBN: 978-1-68401-234-3

www.mascotbooks.com

THE ONE-WEEK-OLD FAWN

A True Story

Best Wishes,
Suzanne M. Malpass

written by

Suzanne M. Malpass

illustrated by

Trish Morgan

Millions of white-tailed deer roam wild around the United States. In the rural area where I live, most people consider them a nuisance. The deer feast on apples, beets, cherries, and corn, as well as many other plants. Sadly, they also sometimes run across the road at the wrong time.

Even so, many people have a soft spot for the little fawns, when they are born each spring. One day, my dog and I shared some close contact with a tiny wild deer and its mother.

Every morning, my Portuguese Water Dog and I go outside to get some exercise. Diva is about ten years old and weighs around forty-five pounds.

Usually we walk in a U-shaped area not far from our house. It's about a mile to the end of the U and back home.

That day, as we approached the far end of the U, a female deer stood there. She was in front of a house with a picket fence. Unlike other deer, this doe didn't race off into the woods as soon as she saw the dog and me.

Instead, she came toward me, turned, and walked away. She did that again and again. "Do you want me to follow you?" I whispered. Finally, I did, and she led me behind some bushes.

Oh, no! Her tiny baby was stuck in the picket fence! The fawn's head and front legs were on one side of the fence, while its tail and back legs were on the other. Its head was down, and its backside was up. As the fawn tried to get free, it kicked up the dirt in front of the fence.

Diva and I ran up to the house to find help. Two cars were in the open garage, and I could hear a T.V. from inside.

I knocked a bunch of times on the door in the garage, but no one ever came. I left the garage, tied Diva to a tree, then hurried back to the baby fawn.

SHRIEK!

Its legs were no bigger around than a thick pencil. I picked up the back legs and tried to help the poor thing out, but the tiny body could not be moved forward or backward.

Suddenly, this little deer had had enough. It let out a short, hugely loud shriek.

Through his open car window, a man must have heard
the sound. He parked his car not far from the doe and me,
then walked toward us.

"The baby is caught in the fence," I said, as I pointed to
the fawn.

The man looked around until he found a rock. With it, he banged the top of one picket free. That made an opening in the fence.

The fawn bounded through the gap and ran off to its mother. They quickly disappeared into the woods.

While the man pounded the picket back into place, I ran to fetch Diva. As we returned, the man said, "I sure hope the little one will be okay. I wonder how long it was trapped."

"Hopefully, not long," I answered. "I read some place that tiny fawns need milk every couple of hours."

A week later, Diva and I were walking our usual route. Once again, we came upon a female deer near the same place as before.

She stared at me. I stared at her. "Are you the one with the little baby? Where **is** your baby?" I asked quietly. I looked all around but could not see a fawn anywhere.

As Diva and I walked on, the doe followed right behind. I could have reached back and touched her. "Is your baby *okay*?" I asked.

We would walk, and she would follow. We would stop, and she would stop. She wasn't afraid of me, and she wasn't afraid of the dog.

The doe kept closely behind us almost all the way home. Then, suddenly, she dashed across the road and went behind some bushes.

A few seconds later, I could see her heading slowly toward the woods. Her sweet little fawn was right behind. Somehow, I felt they had come back to thank me.

Photograph by Gwen Calhoun

Every year, Suzanne M. Malpass and her husband, Jeff Rogers, spend the summer and fall with their dog, Bonita, in Suzanne's hometown of East Jordan, in northwestern lower Michigan. Each winter and spring, they live in their adopted town of Sierra Vista, in southeastern Arizona.

Other books by Suzanne M. Malpass:

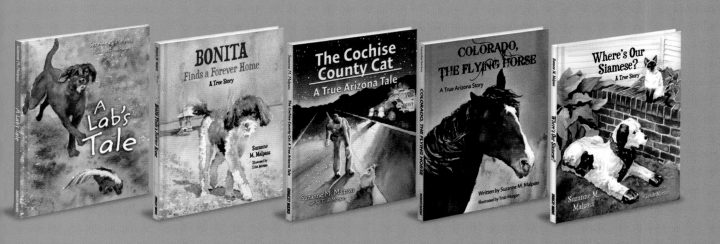